HOCUS

AND

POCUS

AT THE CIRCUS

WEEKLY READER BOOKS PRESENTS

HOCUS AND POCUS
AT THE CIRCUS

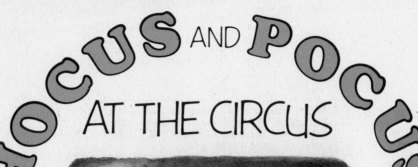

BY FRAN MANUSHKIN
PICTURES BY GEOFFREY HAYES

AN I CAN READ BOOK®

Harper & Row, Publishers

Weekly Reader Books offers several exciting
card and activity programs. For information,
write to WEEKLY READER BOOKS, P.O. Box 16636,
Columbus, Ohio 43216

This book is a presentation of Weekly Reader Books.
Weekly Reader Books offers book clubs for children
from preschool through junior high school.

For further information write to:
Weekly Reader Books
1250 Fairwood Ave.
Columbus, Ohio 43216

Library of Congress Cataloging in Publication Data
Manushkin, Fran.
  Hocus and Pocus at the circus.

  (An I can read book)
  Summary: A young witch tries in vain to teach her
little sister how to spook a Halloween circus.
  [1. Witches—Fiction.   2. Halloween—Fiction.   3. Cir-
cus—Fiction]   I. Hayes, Geoffrey, ill.   II. Title.
III. Series.
PZ7.M3195Ho 1983   [E]   82-47704
ISBN 0-06-024091-1
ISBN 0-06-024092-X (lib. bdg.)

For Nancy Jewell Geller

Hocus and Pocus were witches.

Hocus was mean and nasty.

7

Pocus was her baby sister.

She was learning

to be mean and nasty.

She was not very good at it.

"Tonight is Halloween,"

said Hocus.

"The night to be

mean as a bean."

"Mean, mean, mean!"

chanted Pocus.

"Look at that!" said Hocus.

She pointed to a bright poster.

"Hot apples!" cackled Hocus.

"Let's be mean at the circus."

"Real mean!" said Pocus.

They hopped on their brooms

and flew right over.

All the boys and girls

wore costumes.

There were ballerinas

and clowns

and space monsters too.

"Your witch costumes are very nice,"

said the ticket taker.

"CRACKLE! CRACKLE!"

laughed Hocus and Pocus.

They sat down

in the very first row.

When the lights went out,

Hocus said,

"Now it is time

for you to be mean.

Give this purple candy

to Lola the Lion Tamer."

Pocus ran over

to the lion tamer.

"Purple candy is pretty," said Pocus.

"I'm going to eat it myself."

So she popped the candy

into her mouth.

Instantly,

Pocus turned into a pig!

"OINK!" she squealed.

"GRRR-ROARRRRR!"

roared the lion.

Pocus grabbed his tail

and rode around and around.

"Hooray for the piggy witch!"
cheered the children.

"Cold clams!" yelled Hocus.

"You ruined my spell."

"It was fun," oinked Pocus.

Hocus groaned,

and turned Pocus back

into herself.

"NOW," shouted the Ringmaster,

"HERE ARE

THE BINGLE AND

TINGLE CLOWNS,

THE SILLIEST CLOWNS

IN THE SOLAR SYSTEM!"

"Hooray, hooray!" yelled everyone.

"I'll teach you another way

to spoil the circus,"

said Hocus to Pocus.

"But you must do exactly

what I say.

24

Wave your cape at the clowns

and say, RASTA-FRACH!"

"I'll try it," said Pocus.

The clowns ran out

juggling rubber balls

and dancing with a tiny dog.

"Such a sweet puppy!" cooed Pocus.

She waved her cape

and shouted,

"DOG-A-FRACH!"

Instantly,

all the rubber balls
turned into puppies!

28

Spotted and speckled

and yelping and leaping—

a puppy for everyone

at the circus.

All the children

cheered and cheered.

Hocus moaned and groaned.

"Pocus," she shouted,

"You have to be mean."

"I'm trying," said Pocus.

"I'm trying hard."

"Popcorn! Popcorn!"

called the popcorn lady.

"Now, here's an easy spell,"

said Hocus to Pocus.

"Throw your broom

UP into the air and say—

PEOPLE-CORN! POPPLE-CORN!

Then everyone will turn

into popcorn."

"Oh boy!" said Pocus.

"I want to see THAT!"

She ran around and around, calling,

"PEOPLE-CORN! POPPLE-CORN!"

"I did it right!" she said.

But just then,

she tripped over a puppy

and her broom flew DOWN

instead of UP.

Instantly,

popcorn rained down from above—

warm and buttery

and salted just right.

"Yummmmmm," yelled the children,

as they gobbled it up.

"This circus is magic."

"Dusty kernels," moaned Hocus.

"Can't you do anything right?"

"AND NOW,"

bellowed the Ringmaster,

"HERE ARE THE GREAT

BAMBOOZLES,

THE GREATEST

TRAPEZE ARTISTS

IN THE MILKY WAY!"

"Yaaaaaaaaay!" called the crowd.

Hocus and Pocus ran up

to the trapeze.

"Now," said Hocus to Pocus,

"This is your last chance

to be a mean, mean witch."

"I will try very hard," said Pocus.

"Give this ice cream

to Baby Bamboozle," said Hocus.

"When she eats it,

she will miss her trapeze

and fall to the ground."

"That's too mean!" cried Pocus.

"I will not do it."

Pocus flew away with the ice cream.

Hocus flew after her.

"Give me that cone," she said.

"Here!" said Pocus,

and she poked the cone

into Hocus' mouth!

And

down,

down,

down,

fell Hocus—

right into the cannon!

WHOOOSH!

went Hocus—

right out of the cannon.

"Trick or treat!" shouted Pocus.

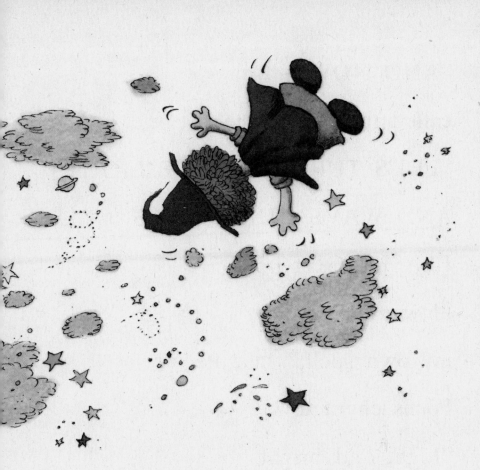

"You mean little witch!"

yelled Hocus.

She flew out of the tent

and out of the circus.

"AND NOW,"

called the Ringmaster,

"LET'S TURN OUT THE LIGHTS

AND WAVE OUR CIRCUS

FLASHLIGHTS."

"I want to try

my own spell," said Pocus.

Pocus chanted,

"Light and bright

and clean as a bean—

happy, happy Halloween!"

Instantly,

all the circus lights

turned into jack-o'-lanterns—

happy, scary faces

flashing bright in the dark.

"Hooray for the little witch!"

everyone shouted.

53

Then they all marched out,
holding their puppies
and waving their pumpkins.

Pocus found her big sister outside,

washing the soot off her face.

"Poor Hocus," said Pocus.

"You didn't have any fun."

"You ruined my Halloween,"

moaned Hocus.

"You turned all my tricks

into treats."

"I like treats!" said Pocus.

"And I have a special one for you."

Pocus waved her arms

and a huge ice-cream cone appeared.

"Is it under a spell?" asked Hocus.

"No," laughed Pocus.

Hocus licked the cone.

"Hot dog!" she said. "I like it.

And I like you too."

"Will you teach me to ride

my broom upside down?"

asked Pocus.

"All right," said Hocus.

And they flew home

by the light

of the Halloween moon.